THE LIAR'S HANDBOOK

KEREN DAVID

Barrington Stoke

First published in 2017 in Great Britain by
Barrington Stoke Ltd
18 Walker Street, Edinburgh, EH3 7LP

www.barringtonstoke.co.uk

Reprinted 2018

A CIP catalogue record for this book is available
from the British Library upon request

ISBN: 978-1-78112-680-6

Printed in China by Leo

For Eliana

CONTENTS

1: DON'T GET ADDICTED TO LYING

My name is River and I am a liar.

Well, that's what everyone else says, anyway.

I don't think that I do lie most of the time. I just think of interesting stuff to say to fill the gaps in what I know.

Here's an example. Last week Miss Shah, my Science teacher, asked where my homework was. I had no idea that she'd even set us any homework. So there was no actual true answer to that question, as my homework had never existed. So technically it wasn't a lie when I told Miss Shah that I'd had a doctor's appointment, but as my doctor is a specialist based off-shore I had to go by helicopter.

And the helicopter pilot had a Doberman puppy and my mum trod on its tail and it nipped her ankle and I used my homework to staunch the flow of blood.

It's not my fault if the rest of the class started laughing and it took Miss Shah ten minutes to calm them down again.

The same rule applies if someone asks where I've been on holiday. We never go anywhere on holiday except to Cornwall and to festivals. So it's not a lie to make something up.

Half of my year still believes that I was a champion snow-boarder at the age of six, and my career was ruined by an encounter with a polar bear during the world junior snow-boarding championships. It was later proved that the bear had been planted on the course by the crazed manager of the Danish team, but by then I'd given up snow-boarding and had a small but vital role in the latest James Bond film, playing an Alsatian. It took hours in costume and make-up.

The other half of my year doesn't believe me even when I do tell the truth. Somehow the truth is never quite enough. No one believed me when I told them I'd learned to surf in Newquay in the summer holidays, even though I'd got really good at it.

But perhaps that was because I also told them that a massive mutant octopus had wrapped its tentacles around my surfboard, but I was lucky and I had a knife on me. (I'd saved an old lady from being mugged earlier that day and hadn't had a chance to hand the thief's blade in to the police.) So I hacked off the tentacles one by one, until the sea churned with blood and bits of octopus and then ...

My stories didn't hurt anyone and I liked how they made me super popular. People called me a legend. I was King of Bants. Even the teachers seemed to look forward to my answer when they asked, "River? What happened this time?"

River is my real name, by the way. No lies there, even though a few years ago I told everyone that my name was actually Egbert Swordhand and I was last in a line descended from the ancient Saxon kings, and my lawyers were preparing a case against the Royal Family for gazillions of pounds.

Four years later, some of the kids at school still call me Eggs.

Anyway, those lies are just one sort of lie. Flights of fancy, my mum calls them. But now I have a mission to complete, and I'm up against someone who tells proper lies all the time. Who's a total fake. And that means I might have to start telling real lies too.

Lies about where I've been and who with. Lies about what I've been up to. Lies about how I feel and what I think. Lies to protect my privacy. Lies to undermine and expose the Enemy.

The Enemy is called Jason. He claims to be in love with my mum. But that's a lie and so is everything else about him.

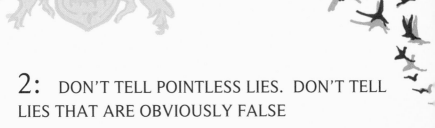

2: DON'T TELL POINTLESS LIES. DON'T TELL LIES THAT ARE OBVIOUSLY FALSE

Mr Zakouri is our Pastoral Head of Year. He doesn't call your parents in to see him unless you're in real trouble or he thinks you need help. Like when my friend Kai got obsessed with looking at stuff online and started being on his phone all the time at school and home. He only escaped total surveillance by joining my football club, so he could prove he was "cutting back on screen time and taking outdoor exercise". Which is great, except the rest of the team sort of blamed me cause Kai is the world's most useless defender (along with the current back line at Arsenal, ha ha). Kai supports Arsenal and I support Spurs, but we can both live with that.

Anyway, I'm sitting in Mr Zakouri's office, waiting for Mum to turn up. Which means I am in deep, deep trouble.

Or I need help. Whatever. I haven't done anything, except tell my Art teacher that Jason is a thief, and he used my sketch book as part of his disguise when he tried to steal the *Mona Lisa*, and that's why it looked like I'd forgotten it.

I mean, it could have been true. Jason says he's a journalist, but he never seems to do any work. And he's never short of money. Maybe he *is* an international art thief.

While we're waiting for Mum, I try and explain to Mr Zakouri where my real dad is.

"He's incredibly busy," I say. "He's in Nigeria."

"Nigeria?" Mr Zakouri says. "Is he from Nigeria?"

"No, he's from Wales," I say.

It might be true. Loads of environmentalists seem to live in Wales – Kai's dad, for example – and one of the only things I know about my dad is that he really cared about the environment.

"There's a crisis in Lagos," I carry on. "He's a trouble-shooter for MI5. He's trying to get some hostages freed. He's, like, an international counter-terrorism expert."

Mr Zakouri sighs and pushes his glasses up his nose. I don't know why he bothers. They slide down again right away.

"Your father works for MI5," he says. "As an agent?"

"Yup."

"River, if that were true, do you think you'd be allowed to tell me about it?"

I think about this. "It could be a sort of double bluff, sir."

"A double bluff?" he says.

"Yup." I nod. "Like, because I tell you about it, you think it can't be true, but actually it is."

"So that's why your father's not been to a single parents' evening since you joined the school?" Mr Zakouri says.

"He's way too busy, sir."

Mr Zakouri shakes his head. "Oh, dear," he says, then the door opens and Mum comes in.

My mum always looks amazing. She makes all her own clothes from stuff she gets from charity shops. She likes bright colours, so today she's got on a sunshine yellow top, with sleeves covered in pink roses. Her shoes are a green shiny material which looks like silk but isn't, because it's cruel to exploit silkworms. Her orange skirt puffs out at the sides. Her silver hoop earrings are the size of saucers, standing out against her dark skin and black hair. Her eyelids shine and her lips glitter with gloss. I look at her and I know that she's dressed for a fight. And my mum tends to win fights.

"Mrs Jones," Mr Zakouri says.

"*Ms* Jones," she replies. "But you can call me Tanya."

Mr Zakouri nods. "Ms Jones – Tanya – River has just informed me that his father is in Nigeria to resolve a hostage crisis. Is that true?"

Mum's mouth twitches. "No," she says. "River, why would you say that?"

I shrug. "He might be," I say.

"Ms Jones." Mr Zakaouri sounds like he means business. "I've asked you here today because we're worried about River's behaviour. His imagination seems to be out of control. He tells lie after lie after lie."

"Oh, River," Mum says. "Not again."

"I don't think it's a problem," I tell her.

"We're worried that River can't tell fact from fiction," Mr Zakouri says. "He's turning into a Walter Mitty."

"A what?" Mum says.

"Walter Mitty," Mr Zakouri says. "Famous fictional character who lived in a fantasy world. Invented by James Thurber, played by Danny Kaye in the 1940s film and in a 2013 remake by Ben Stiller. But it wasn't a patch on the original."

Mum glowers at Mr Zakouri. "You're comparing my son to a made-up character? And you say *he* can't tell fact from fiction?"

I sneak Mum a little *thank you* smile. She gives me a *wait till we get home* glare.

But Mr Zakouri glowers straight back at Mum. "Ms Jones," he says. "I think you know as well as I do that River's got a problem. He's more than old enough to know what's true and what's not."

Mum sighs. "I'm sorry, Mr Zakouri. I thought River had grown out of telling stories. But does it matter so much? There's so much more in the world to worry about."

"Such as?" Mr Zakouri asks.

Mum doesn't miss a beat. "The environment. Politics. War. Poverty. Refugees. I mean, is it surprising that some people retreat into fantasy?"

"You think River's lies are a reaction to global events?" Mr Zakouri says. "Is that true, River?"

I shake my head.

"Well," Mr Zakouri says. "We've got a plan. River, your English teacher thinks you've got a fantastic flair for story-telling. Here's an exercise book. Why don't you write down all the tall tales you can think of? Write them down instead of trying to convince people that they're true."

I open my mouth and then close it again.

"Lying is a fine art, River," Mr Zakouri says. "At the moment you're not very good at it. Consider yourself warned."

Mum ignores the warning. "That's a good idea, Mr Zakouri," she says. "You can write about our holiday in Costa Rica, can't you, River?"

"Costa Rica?" Mr Zakouri parrots. He looks like he thinks Mum is the one telling stories now.

But Mum's on a roll, telling Mr Zakouri all about our 'special holiday'. All the bio-diversity and special conservation stuff. All the people

Jason is going to interview for *National Geographic*. Allegedly.

All the stuff I don't believe and don't want to know about.

So I shut my ears and close my eyes. And I think about this stupid book. It's not going to be stories I tell instead of lies. It's going to be a guidebook – a book of instructions for telling lies.

It's going to be called *The Liar's Handbook*.

3: TELL TOO MANY LIES AND NO ONE BELIEVES IT WHEN YOU TELL THE TRUTH

It's 5.05 a.m. and we're at the airport. Jason's gone off to buy coffees and I'm arguing with Mum.

"I just said that if Jason really cared about the environment then we wouldn't be getting a plane all the way to Costa Rica."

"You called him a fake," Mum says for the second time.

"He is a fake."

"So am I a fake too?" Mum demands. "Because I'm getting on this plane too, River."

"Can I stay at home?" I say. "I could go to Kai's house."

"No! No you cannot!" Mum almost shouts. "Why do you have to be like this?"

"Why do *you* have to be like this?"

She tries a different tack, her voice soft now. Too soft. "I know it's scary, River, flying for the first time."

"I'm not scared! At least not for me. I'm thinking about the planet! What about our carbon footprint?"

"River," she sighs. "I haven't been on a plane for years. Not since I left New Zealand. And this is a very special trip, darling."

I don't need her *special*. "I could stay at home," I say. "You and Jason would have a better time by yourselves."

"But I want you there," she says, not giving up. "And for you to get to know Jason. Believe me, River, he's someone you can trust."

"Yeah, right. You're really good at finding the ones to trust, aren't you?"

Mum blinks. She looks hurt. I feel mean and bad and angry that I've been forced into a position where I say things like that to her. It's all Jason's fault. But she doesn't think so.

"There's no need for that, River," she says. "That's not fair."

It's not fair that you've decided to import Jason into our tiny house, I want to say. It's not fair that you made that decision on your own. It's not fair that you and he have secrets, so you shut up when I come into the room. It's not fair that sometimes he makes you cry and you won't tell me why.

"Nothing's fair," I say. "Life's not fair."

"I just wish we could ..." Her voice trails off. "Trust me, River. Jason's a nice guy. More than nice."

Jason comes back then with the coffees so I don't have to answer. I take my drink, turn my back, plug myself into my headphones and lose myself in music.

There's no way I could ever trust Jason. He isn't "nice". The word for him is smooth. From his smooth, posh voice to his smooth, shiny hair. (I know he uses conditioner! Probably not even organic!) His smooth, pale skin. His smart, ironed jeans. His crisp polo shirts.

And the smooth way he ignores my insults, and pretends to be interested in me, and asks me about school and football and friends and all that stuff that is actually none of his business.

And the smooth way he persuaded Mum to get engaged – to *marry* him one day. I've sworn that will never, ever happen.

4: EVERYONE TELLS LIES

Costa Rica. Day 2.

Yesterday we toured a rain forest conservation project. It would have been very interesting if I hadn't been on high alert the whole time watching Jason and Mum to monitor their relationship.

It's difficult to find any proof that Jason is a liar, a con man, a big, fat fake. He asks the tour guide clever questions. He looks concerned about rare reptiles that are about to become extinct.

I was beginning to think it was all OK. They'd come to their senses.

But now it's Day 2, I've just come down for breakfast and I'm looking at someone who might be, who could be ...

Kai!

He's just standing in the middle of the hotel lobby, looking shifty.

I can't believe my eyes! Does Kai have some sort of Costa Rican lookalike? The real Kai told me he was going to Liverpool to see his nan.

"Hey, Kai," I say, all casual, just in case I've totally forgotten a conversation in which he said, "By the way, we're coming to Costa Rica too."

"Hey, bro."

We stand there trying to think of what to say next. It's all a bit awkward, then Kai says, "See the fixtures for next season?" and I say, "Yeah, Finchley Barbarians Under 16s first week." Then we both shake our heads and make "I'm in pain" faces, because the Barbarians are complete monsters and last season they beat us into second place in the North London U15 Sunday League (division 6). Now we're both in division 5, so it's a whole new ball game.

That is, it's the same ball game but with bigger opponents, a bigger pitch, a bigger goal and 40 minutes each half.

Then Kai's mum Lorna finishes talking to the guy at the hotel desk, and she comes over and says, "Surprise! I bet we're the last people you expected to see! Talk about romantic!"

And I shrug and say, "Yeah?" I have no idea what she's on about.

And Kai says, "It would be really cool if we didn't have to go to this stupid wedding."

"Oh, Kai!" Lorna tuts. "Don't be like that. It's River's mum's big day!"

"Big day? You what?" I manage.

"A wedding on the beach!" Lorna cries. "So dreamy! So romantic!"

Right up to this point I've always thought that Lorna was a sensible sort of person. Dental nurses have to have their wits about them, just in case someone randomly bites them. (I may have done this when I was five. I can't remember if it was just a story or not. I think I did it, but the gushing blood and the life-threatening infection that the dentist got probably weren't true.)

But it soon turns out Lorna isn't very sensible at all.

She goes on and on ... the flowers, the dress, the top secret invite from Jason, along with plane tickets and the hotel all paid for.

"What a gem!" she gushes. "Lucky Tanya!"
It was all so secret that she didn't even tell Kai
where they were going until they were boarding
the plane.

"I would've warned you if I'd known," he tells
me when his mum goes skipping off to the loo.

"What's your dad going to say about this?"
I ask him. Kai's dad is really old school. He's
been away for months, on a boat in the Arctic,
protesting about oil drilling.

"He's not going to be impressed that we flew
here," Kai says.

He's right. When his dad went to Australia for
a conference on sustainability, he didn't catch a
single plane. The trip took him eight months.

"Ah well, mate," I say. "See you later. I'm on a
mission to stop a wedding."

I bash on Mum and Jason's door as loud as I
can.

At last Mum opens it. "River," she says, and
then she sees my face. "Oh, darling. What's
happened?"

"What's happened? Only Kai turning up and
telling me he's here for a wedding!"

"Oh sweetheart – River –"

"When were you thinking of telling me?"

"Soon," she says. "I mean, you knew we were engaged, you knew it was happening one day –"

"Not today!"

"Friday," she corrects me. "And it's really small. Just us and Lorna and Kai. Wasn't it nice of Jason to invite them? So kind."

Nice – that word again. *Kind.*

"He's what I need," Mum says. *Yuck.* "Be nice for me, darling. One day you'll understand."

One day you'll understand. Probably the most infuriating words any parent can say to any child. My mum used to be more like a friend than a mum. A best friend. Someone who shared everything with me. I could have a laugh with her, share a room with her on holiday, tell her stuff.

Jason's changed all that. OK, I got older too, but it's mostly Jason.

But I can't make a fuss at the wedding. Mum'd be so upset. Instead I get my hopes up that it's not even legal in the UK. I googled it and it seems that beach weddings abroad are pretty flaky.

It's a big, fat, fake wedding for a big, fat, fake fiancé. (Fat is a metaphor here. Jason's not fat in reality. He's six foot one and has been flaunting his six pack at the pool all week. Kai's too intimidated to take off his T-shirt.)

So that's how I end up standing on a burning hot beach a few days later watching Mum in a bright pink dress listen to vows made up by Jason. He looks ridiculous in a pale pink shirt and cream trousers.

"You two! So glam!" Lorna said when they came down to the beach, but Kai and I just rolled our eyes at each other.

Mum looks so happy. No frown on her face. No shadows under her eyes. I can't wipe that megawatt smile off her face. I have to be a hero, and put my own feelings aside.

Jason tried to apologise a few days ago. "Sorry, mate," he said. "I should have asked your permission. I was just worried that you'd say no."

"Yeah," I replied. "You should have."

He didn't take the hint. "I'd like to think that we had your blessing," he went on. "I love your mum, so much. And to be part of a family –"

"Whatever," I said, and walked off.

I'm in my long-sleeved T-shirt and my jeans, even though it's crazy hot and everyone laughed when they saw me. I'm not going to risk skin cancer any more than I need to.

I want to shout, "Don't trust him!"

I want to shout, "He'll break your heart!"

I want to shout, "He'll leave you!"

But I don't. Because my mum knows all that and she's still doing it anyway.

It's like she's forgotten what happened with my dad.

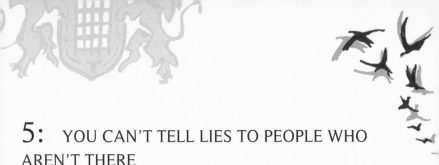

5: YOU CAN'T TELL LIES TO PEOPLE WHO AREN'T THERE

My dad's name is Matthew Jordan. He first met Mum a year before I was born, at a festival in Somerset, also known as the middle of nowhere.

There's a photo of him at the festival, with fields and tatty tents in the background. His dusty dreadlocks are a faded orange colour like a fox, and he has blue eyes and a small snubby nose. On his arm is a tattoo of a red rose in a spider's web.

It seems he played the guitar and sang folk songs, Mum's favourites, and he made her laugh. "I saw him and I just knew," is what she told me.

They stayed up all night every night talking. They danced together as the sun rose. They believed in the same things – a cleaner, kinder, safer world. They knew that you have to fight for those things. And when Mum went back to her bedsit in Clapton, Matthew Jordan came with her.

They were both alone in the world. When she was sixteen, Mum had fled her children's home in New Zealand to backpack her way round the world. Ten years later, she pitched up in England. Her motto is "Never look back".

If it hadn't been for Dad and then me, she might still be travelling now.

My dad didn't want to talk about his family at all. He hardly ever mentioned his past. "You're all I need, Tanya," he'd say. "You are my everything."

He got cash-in-hand jobs on building sites, and he joined in with Mum's world. He met her activist friends and worked with them, doing everything they could to save the Earth from pollution and greenhouse gases and global warming. He wrote leaflets and handed them out and went on protests. Other stuff as well. Direct action. Matthew helped plan the invasion of the BBC newsroom, which was the first time Mum got arrested. He threw a party for her and her friend Ruth when they got out of prison after the protest at the nuclear power station.

"You're my hero!" he told her. "We're going to save this planet together!"

That was good Matthew. Nice Matthew. Kind Matthew. But there was another side to him. Sad Matthew. Moody Matthew. Depressed Matthew. When he felt dark like that he would leave. Sometimes for a day, sometimes for a week. Mum didn't like it, but she got used to it. He'd always come back. He'd apologise and say he wasn't good enough for her, and he'd cry and she'd cry and they'd make up.

Except one time, he didn't come back. Not for one week, two weeks, six weeks. Not ever.

Mum hadn't even told him she was pregnant.

6: FOOTBALL IS A BREEDING GROUND FOR LIES

So we've been back from Costa Rica for three weeks and today is the first day of the football season. Jason's insisting that he comes with me to watch us play the Finchley Barbarians.

You'd think he'd have taken the hint by now that I have no interest at all in him as my step-dad. I've dropped enough clues. But no, he's super keen and refuses to let me put him off, in a way that I find frankly creepy.

I've tried some lies. I told him that parents aren't allowed at our matches, after a game last season when Hakim's dad hit the linesman after he ruled Hakim's goal offside.

"It's probably different now you're in the Under 16s," Jason said.

I told him that I'd be on the bench for most of the match as we have too many star strikers.

"That's OK," he said. "We can watch together."

I told him the pitch would be a mud bath, there were no toilets and it was going to rain. Actually, none of that was lies.

"That's OK," he said again. He was so annoying. "I've got wellies, an umbrella and the bladder of a camel."

I never knew that camels were famous for their bladder control, but in the car Jason tells me that he once ran a marathon in the Sahara (an obvious lie), and he learned how camels only pee once a week. When they do pee, their pee is thick as syrup. Then he said that some people believe that camel pee can cure you of cancer if you drink it. And that camels can go for days without drinking anything and then drink almost 200 litres of water all in one go. And that camels can kick all four of their legs in four different directions at once.

Huh. And they call me a liar.

"Let's hope the other team haven't signed a camel over the summer," Jason says, as we park by the playing fields the Barbarians use as their home pitch.

"It'd be against Sunday League regulations," I say, to shut him up. "Can we park the car further away?"

"Why?"

"Because Mum might have forgotten that we don't approve of cars, but I haven't."

"Oh. Sorry," Jason says. "But didn't you notice that it's electric? Zero emission? Voted Best New Green Car in the World last year?"

Him and his fake electric car. It's got a petrol cap on the side.

"Just move it round the corner, OK?" I say.

By the time Jason makes it out to the pitch I've told the whole team and Marcus-the-Manager that some smarmy guy has been bothering me, asking questions and inviting me back to his place. When Jason arrives, asking cheerily if there's anything he can do to help, I hiss, "That's him! Call the police!"

But Marcus says, "Don't be daft, River, we've all seen your mum's wedding pictures on Facebook. Come off it." He shakes Jason's hand and says, "Congratulations, mate. You've pulled a cracker with that Tanya. Good luck with young River, eh? You'll need it."

"Oh, I don't think so," Jason says. He smiles his stupid smile and pumps Marcus's hand up and down. "Who are we playing today then?"

Next thing I know, Marcus has recruited Jason as assistant manager. Without even asking me! And now he's briefing him about the strengths and weaknesses of our team and the dangers posed by the Barbarians.

"I've heard they've got a couple of new players," Marcus says. "There's a boy with ginger hair, plays left wing, makes Usain Bolt look sluggish. And their new goalie is built like a tank. Here they come now. See him?"

He's not wrong. The boy is massive. He must be over six foot tall. His chest is as wide as the fridge that Jason's installed in our old spare room, so he can have a beer when he's pretending to work. I'd like a fridge like that, if fridges weren't so bad for the environment. Anyway, the gigantic goalie's arms are as long as a gorilla's (but not as hairy) and his legs are as solid as an elephant's (but only two of them, not four). I'm thinking how it's a good job the Under 16s play with a full-size goal, because this boy would spill out of anything smaller.

Half our team want to call him the Hulk. The other half prefer Hagrid. As captain I'm about to cast the deciding vote, when Jason interrupts.

"Don't give him a name that makes him sound powerful," he says. "Call him Butter Fingers, or Ball Dropper, or Meat Hands, or …"

"Meat Hands!" Kai yells at the Barbarians goalie.

"Butter Fingers!"

"Ball Dripper!"

"Ball Dropper," I mutter, cross.

Jason winks at me. I ignore him. Has he no dignity?

The whistle blows and the match starts. I'm desperate to perform well. I run like the wind up and down the pitch. I pass, back and forward. I send a flurry of good clean balls into the box, but my team mates fail to follow through. The Barbarians make it one–nil (that's the fast ginger guy on the left wing), and then two–nil (him again). Fifteen minutes to half time.

This time I dribble the ball up field myself, rather than risk passing again. I dodge past one defender, two defenders, a quick one–two, past defender number three, pull my boot back, ready to strike and – *WHAM!* – I go splat into the massive goalie, who's rushing to clear the ball.

"PENALTY!" I yell before I fall onto the pitch, holding my head.

"I GOT THE BALL!" Hagrid the Hulk shouts, as his nose spurts blood everywhere.

The referee blows his whistle, shouts for First Aid and awards a goal kick.

"PENALTY!" I scream.

It's so unfair. As the home side, the Barbarians have to provide the ref and at least one linesman. Jason's running the other line. Of course the ref is going to be biased towards their side, just as Max's dad is when we play at our home ground.

"First Aid!" the ref shouts. "Let's get these boys sorted out."

So I have to be substituted and so does Hagrid the goalie. Our sub, Sonny, is super happy to see me come off. The Hulk has to strip off his goalie top to give to the boy coming on, and when he takes it off you can see that a lot of that impressive bulk is just plain old flab, covered with goose-pimples in the cold wind.

The top swamps the boy who puts it on. He turns a bit green as he pulls it over his head, as it's sweaty and specked with Hulkish blood.

"Do I have to wear it?" he moans, and the Hulk crosses his arms and looks embarrassed because there's no way he can fit into the other boy's top. His nose is still flowing as he struggles into his hoodie.

You'd never have thought a snubby little nose like that could bleed so much.

My nose is almost the same shape, and when it bleeds it's like turning on a tap. My nose just isn't built for pinching, and nor is Hagrid the Hulk's. His dad's trying to get a grip on it, but he's just getting in a mess.

"Don't worry, Ollie old chap," I hear him say. "You were doing great out there. And it was clear you got the ball. It was no penalty."

On the pitch, Sonny scores an easy chip over the new goalie's head.

I hardly notice, because I'm glaring at Hagrid's dad. How's his son meant to learn the rules of football with that sort of advice?

And then I see it.

On his right arm. Just above the hand that grips his son's nose. A tattoo of a red rose inside a spider's web.

I've seen that tattoo before, and not because it's a common design.

My dad had that tattoo on his arm too.

7: LIARS NEED GOOD FRIENDS

I don't tell Kai there and then because I'm too gob-smacked. Also he's still on the pitch, playing.

Plus, after half time I'm subbed back on again (Kai comes off), and so is the Hulk. I take great joy in smashing the winning goal past him with a stunning kick from the centre line.

OK, not quite from the centre line. But pretty far out. And OK, the equaliser, not the actual winning goal, but it feels like a victory. The final result is 4–4.

I watch Hagrid the Hulk and his dad leave. My head's in a whirl.

That man has my dad's tattoo. The tattoo is on all three of the photos of him that my mum has. She says he didn't like having his picture taken.

His nose is small and snubby just like my dad's.

He has reddish hair, just like my dad.

But this man's hair is short and neat, he drives a gas-guzzling BMW, he's wearing chinos and I'd heard him at half time discussing Arsenal's chances for the season. Mum says my dad had no interest in football – I'd asked her a few times which team he supported.

But maybe he got interested in the last few years. And maybe he's now the sort of guy who drives cars that use up the Earth's resources and pollute the air. And anyone could get a nerdy haircut and take to wearing stupid clothes.

Is it him?

Have I found my dad?

No, I can't have.

His son, the Hulk, must be pretty much the same age as me. So maybe I've found my dad's brother. They could have got the tattoos done together. Maybe they were part of some secret society or a criminal gang and the tattoo was their sign.

Maybe Dad was on the run when he met Mum, and that's why he disappeared.

And maybe his brother is a master criminal, and I need to tread very carefully from now on.

On the way home, Jason wants to do a post-match analysis, but I insist on sitting in the back of the car so I can message Kai in private.

> You got to keep this top secret OK?

> OK

> You know Hagrid?

> Who?

> Their goalie. Tank boy.

> Oh yeah. Ball Dropper. Ha ha. He's a laugh your new dad.

> That name was pathetic. Plus he's not my dad.

> OK, yeah, pathetic. You're right.

Anyway, I need to investigate Hagrid's dad.

?????

Because he has the same tattoo as my real dad.

You think he's your dad?

I don't know.

That would make you and Hagrid BROTHERS? That's weird even for you.

We're NOT brothers. Cousins maybe.

Did you ask?

Of course not! Are you mad?

"All right in the back?" Jason interrupts. "Shall we stop and get fish and chips for lunch?"

"No," I say. "We're vegan. I thought you were too."

The back of his neck goes red. "Oh, err, yes, I am. Just a bit new to it, that's all."

"I've never eaten any animal products," I tell him.

"Good for you."

"Mum wouldn't like it if you took fish and chips home."

"No. Thanks for the warning, eh?"

Warning?

I've totally messed up. I should've said yes to the fish and chips and then Mum would realise that Jason's concern for the environment, for the planet, for animals and everything else about him is totally, completely, absolutely fake.

"Whatever," I say, and I go back to messaging Kai.

> We need to track my dad down. Warn him.

> Warn him about what?

Warn him that I've found his evil brother who's the head of a criminal gang.

Eh?

What are you doing later? I'll explain.

BBQ. You're coming.

No way. You're roasting hunks of animal flesh on an open fire? Caveman or what?

You are coming. Mum asked your mum and Jason. And you, obvs. She's got veggie sausages and everything.

OK, see you later.

CU.

No one does that text speak thing any more. Only parents.

Soz.

8: PEOPLE LIE TO BE LIKED

The smell of burning flesh at the barbeque is distracting, but I manage to fill Kai in. Mind you, I enjoy the look on Jason's face as he pretends to enjoy his charred veggie sausage.

Several of Mum's friends are here, all eating veggie sausages. They're talking about the old days when they were all part of an activist group. Mum and Lorna. Kai's dad, Kevin. Sean and Luisa and Anders. And my dad – Matthew. Everyone's here except Kai's dad and mine. At least Kai has an idea where his dad is. At least he knows his dad hasn't given up on fighting for a better world.

Mum does her fighting with words now. She writes leaflets and reports for a charity, Planet Positive. Most of the rest of them do some stuff – they're vegan, they recycle, they vote Green – but now they have boring, ordinary jobs like teacher and gardener and dental nurse. Kai's step-dad is called Bob and he's a builder. That's true.

Jason's asking them about the old days.

"We were serious about stuff back then," Kai's mum says. "We were willing to risk it all. Remember that sit-in, Tanya? At the site of the Sheringham bypass?"

"We won that battle," Mum says, "but did we win the war? Politicians say they care about the environment, but it's all empty words. All they care about is money and power."

"But you're doing so much to change things," Jason says. She smiles and strokes his arm. It's like they can't keep their hands off each other. It's disgusting.

"Direct action felt so good," she says. "Now we spend our time asking for support, trying to change the way laws are made. It's legal and sensible and right ... but our planet is still dying."

"You're doing more than you realise," Jason tells her. "You don't have to shout to be heard, when the things you say are true and important."

"Aw," Kai's mum says. "You two are so good together."

Jason goes a bit red, and he pushes his shiny hair out of his eyes. "I mean it," he says.

"That's not what my dad thinks," Kai says.

Puzzled, Jason looks over at Bob the Builder, who's stuffing his mouth full of dead cow.

"Kai means my ex," Lorna says. "Last of the hardcore headbangers. Right now on a protest boat in the Arctic. We're hoping he doesn't get arrested."

"He won't – will he?" Kai asks. "Dad knows what he's doing. He's already got so much publicity!"

"Kevin MacDougall," Mum tells Jason. "He and Matthew were good mates."

"They were, weren't they?" Lorna says. "But I still can't believe Matthew just up and left like that ..."

"It was a long time ago," Mum says firmly.

"Yes, and it'll be a long time before Kai sees his dad again," Lorna says. "Last time he pulled a stunt like this he spent six weeks in prison in Alaska."

Kai's getting het up. "It's not a stunt, Mum," he says. "Dad's a proper eco warrior! Not like you, eating meat and wearing leather shoes and leaving all the lights on ..."

"OK, OK," says Lorna.

"The boy's not wrong," Sean says.

I don't like Sean. He takes everything on the nose, as if he's always gunning for a scrap. Plus, he's mean to my mum. He says she's sold out. He thinks – Mum told me once – that she drove my dad away.

"They *were* good mates," she says. "Kevin never forgave me for letting Matthew go. Not that I had a choice in the matter."

"My dad's a proper warrior," Kai says again.

But Sean just shakes his head, takes a drag on his roll-up and says, "Protests are only a step up from shuffling papers." He looks over at Mum and starts to rant. "What difference will they make out on their boat? Politicians treat us with pure contempt. They think they can get away with anything. You've got to hit people where it hurts. Make them listen. Let them know you'll fight to the bitter end."

Lorna's uncomfortable. I can tell by the way she says, "Anyone want any more salad?"

Mum is glad of the chance to jump up and help. "I'll stick some more black-bean burgers on the barbie, shall I?" she says.

But Jason turns to Sean. "I know what you mean, mate," he says. "Sometimes the only way is to take the law into your own hands."

I can't stand his fakeness any more.

I nudge Kai. "Come on, eco warrior," I say. "Let's take the bottles to the recycling bank."

As we lug the two heavy bags of bottles along, I brief Kai about the tattoo.

Then we take turns dropping the bottles into the bank.

"OK, so you need to find out a whole load more about your dad," Kai says.

SMASH!

"Mum doesn't seem to know much."

CRASH!

"You know his name, don't you? And when he was born?"

SMASH!

"Yes, but I don't know anything else. Like where he was from or anything."

CRASH!

"I think you can get hold of his birth certificate if you have a name and date of birth," Kai says. "Assuming he was born in this country."

CRASH!

"How will that help?" I ask.

SMASH!

"It'll tell you his parents' names and their address when he was born. And then you can find out if he has any brothers or sisters."

CRASH!

"Kai, you are a genius. How did you know about that?"

SMASH!

"My grandad's into family history. He's traced us back to 1700 and something. My great-great-great-grandad was a blacksmith. You just apply for the documents online."

CRASH!

"Awesome! You get the last three bottles. Let's go for it."

SMASH! CRASH! SMASH!

9: REAL LIARS FAKE EVERYTHING

Mum and Jason are going out for a drink.

"What about River?" I hear her say.

"He'll be OK," Jason says. "To be honest, Tanya, I need a night off from the constant hostility."

"Shh," she says. "He'll come round. It's just been the two of us for a long time. Me and him. All his life, in fact."

"If I could just talk to him –"

"One day. Hang in there, darling."

I don't need to look to know that they're kissing. Revolting.

Then they head out and I'm all alone with a bowl of brown rice and butterbean stew.

I polish that off, and then I find the box with my dad's passport. He even left that behind.

There he is, with his ratty dreads and his beard and his little round glasses. He looks nothing like Hagrid the goalie's dad.

Except for his nose.

There's his name – Matthew Peter Jordan.

There's his place of birth – London.

And his date of birth – 07/03/1973

I read it all, just like I've read it a thousand times. And I wonder, just like I always do – why would you disappear and leave your passport behind? It's clear he didn't mean to disappear. It's clear he was on the run from his brother and his criminal gang. Or whatever.

Whatever ... but I never ever let myself think that my dad might have been murdered. It takes a lot of effort to block that idea.

I message all the details to Kai and then I head upstairs. Time to investigate Jason's stuff. I'm looking for anything which shows him up as a fake. And I'm interested to know how he paid for a trip to Costa Rica for five.

That's the easiest one to answer. I find some folders with bank statements in and have a look. Jason has a ton of money and a few different bank accounts. Loads of money in his savings accounts – I add it up to over £20,000. And £5,000 in a couple of current accounts too.

I also find a file about a flat in Holland Park, which is a part of London where you only live if you're rich enough to own a football club. And this flat seems to belong to Jason because there's a letter from an estate agent valuing it at a cool two million quid. For a flat. A not even very swanky two-bed flat.

So. Maybe Jason's a drug dealer. Maybe he's an international jewel thief. Maybe he's like those guys on *The Secret Millionaire*, except none of them get married before they hand out wads of cash to poor people. I'm pretty sure he doesn't own a football club, but you never know. Maybe he's a Russian billionaire in disguise.

But if he's so rich why has he moved in here, to our tiny house where we are all falling over each other?

He's had to put his computer in our spare room, which is too small to even be a proper spare room. The room's now full of Jason's desk and Jason's computer, Jason's beer fridge and Jason's box files full of articles he's written with neat labels on. Motorway schemes. Power stations. New developments. An extra runway at Manchester airport. Toad habitats. Polar bears. Bees.

I switch on his computer. I guess his password (*Tanya* plus the date of their fake beach wedding), and I'm in.

I click on lots of random stuff and it's all pretty boring. He's even gone to the trouble of faking a load of photos of the Sahara marathon, with him cosying up to camels. They must have been taken in a zoo. A very sandy zoo.

I'm about to give up, when I see it. Lurking in a folder called 'admin'. There's another folder and it's called Jordan. My dad's name. Jordan.

Of course, it could be Jordan the country. Or Jordan the trainers.

I click on the folder.

Oh.

It's not Jordan the country.

It's not Jordan the trainers.

It's totally about my dad. Photos of him from years ago. Newspaper cuttings of him on protests. A whole file of interviews with people who knew him. I scan these first.

"Matt was a great geezer. Life and soul of the party. Everyone loved him."

"You'd follow Matt to the ends of the earth. Maybe that's why we did some of the crazy stuff that we did."

"He was always full of ideas – he was the one who said we should break into the power station, who got us the wire cutters and posters. But it was Tanya and Anders who got arrested. Matt cried off at the last minute."

"He was the brains and we were the soldiers."

"He gave me strength. He'd talk to me like I really mattered and then I'd feel on top of the world, like I could make a difference."

"What can I say? Matthew was one of a kind."

"Sometimes I look back and wonder, *Was he just telling us what to do?*"

"Why did he disappear?"

"Why did he disappear?"

"Why did he disappear?"

As I read all this, I feel proud and sad and confused and angry – how dare Jason snoop into my dad's life? I read it again. I think about printing it out, but then I worry Jason will find out. Instead I email a copy to myself. Then I worry that Jason will trace that on his computer. I feel sick, and my hands are all sweaty.

Then I hear their voices. I sneak a look out of the window. They're sitting on the bench and Jason has his arm round my mum.

I can't get caught snooping. I close the file and shut down the computer. I put the box files back in order again. I worry that my sweaty hands have left marks on the boxes, that I have messed up somehow, that Jason will realise what I've done. But it was so worth it. I've found out so many secrets.

Jason's rich.

Jason's nosy.

Jason's far too interested in my dad.

What if he's part of a criminal gang that's after my dad? He hasn't got a tattoo that I know about, but you can have them lasered off. Or maybe this is the job that he has to do to join the gang. What if his instructions are –

"Matthew Jordan is a traitor. Track him down and assassinate him and his family!"

I was right to call Jason the Enemy.

He's seriously dangerous.

And I need to find out more about my dad before he does.

10: SOMETIMES THE TRUTH IS EASIER

Kai rings me on Saturday. "Get yourself down here," he says. "The birth certificate's arrived."

When I get there his mum and Bob the Builder are working in their garden.

"Hi, River." Lorna waves at me.

"Hey, kid," says Bob.

I wave back and head for Kai's room.

"Here it is," he says, and he hands over a brown envelope.

It's strange to see my dad's name in black and white on an official document. If I add this to the passport, it nearly makes a whole person.

The information on the birth certificate is –

Date of birth – *07/03/1973*

Place of birth – *Homerton, London*

Forename(s) – *Matthew Peter*

Sex – *Male*

Name and surname of Father – *Peter Jordan*

Name, surname and maiden surname of Mother – *Elizabeth Jordan (née Lacey)*

Occupation of Father – *Bus driver*

Signature, description and residence of informant – *Peter Jordan, Father, 54 Rathbone Gardens, Ilford, Essex*

When registered – *09/03/1973*

The thin paper shakes in my hand as I read it. I have almost nothing from my dad, nothing, and now all this. All these facts. I imagine my grandad, driving his bus around the streets of Ilford. I imagine Peter Jordan getting married to Elizabeth – no, Lizzy. Lizzy Lacey and Pete Jordan. Happy ever after. And then they have two boys, and one is called Matthew and he has a son called River. And that's me, and they don't even know me.

I wonder if they're still alive. I wonder if they still live in Ilford. I wonder if I've ever got on a bus driven by my grandad, paid him my fare and said "thank you" as I got off, and neither of us knew the other.

Imagine! But what if I'd got on a bus and looked at the driver and somehow recognised him? What if he had a spider-rose tattoo on his arm? What if I said, "Hello, I'm River," and he said, "I know. I've been waiting to meet you."

But my dad doesn't even know that he's my dad, so that's not very likely.

But this birth certificate is a massive step nearer to finding him. Or at least it could be.

"Let's look on Google maps," Kai says, like he can read my mind.

Google maps swoops in on London ... Ilford ... Rathbone Gardens. And there it is. A little house, stuck to the house next door. A red front door. If you zoom right in you can see some gnomes in the front garden.

"Wow," I say. I'm giddy, as though I've actually flown to Rathbone Gardens and zoomed in on the gnomes myself.

"I bet they still live there," Kai says.

He turns the image back into a map, zooms out, finds the nearest tube station. It's just around the corner from the house where my dad might have grown up. We look up the map of the

London Underground – it's on the Central Line.
If we get the Victoria Line to Oxford Circus and
change, we could go there. We could take a look.

"You doing anything this afternoon?" says Kai.

"I am now," I reply.

It takes us forty minutes to get to Rathbone
Gardens. We're hot and hungry, because we
forgot to have lunch. Kai looks with longing at
a Burger King by the station (their fries are the
best), but I drag him away.

And now we're standing outside a little house,
feeling completely stupid.

"Shall we knock?" Kai says. "After we've come
all this way?"

"No," I say. "I mean, yes. I mean no.
Definitely no." I don't move.

"We should just ask," he says. "Go on, think of
a cover story. You're good at stories."

It's funny how you can't drum up lies when
you need them. My mind is a blank.

"We could say ... we're doing a survey for a
Geography project," I say at last.

"A survey of what?"

"Ages," I say. "We have to find out the ages of everyone in the street and then work out the mean, median and mode."

"Pathetic."

"Can you think of anything better?"

"Collecting for charity?"

We get half way up the path – there are the gnomes and a little statue of a pixie – before I get cold feet.

"I can't do it!" I tell Kai.

"You can! Go on!"

We're still arguing when the door opens. An old lady looks out at us. "Do you want something, boys?" she asks.

I'm struck dumb. She has to be Lizzy Jordan. She's just the right age.

"We're collecting –" Kai starts, but I step on his toes.

"Are you Mrs Jordan?" I ask. I'm trying to smile. I'm trying to look like the sort of boy you'd want as a grandson.

"I am indeed," she replies.

11: LIES CAN'T GET YOU OUT OF TROUBLE ALL THE TIME

Mrs Jordan is looking nervous, wary, on edge. I try and relax, so she'll trust me. I want her to like me.

"What can I do for you?" she asks. "How do you know my name?"

"I was wondering." I pause. How to put it? "Did you have a son called Matthew?"

She looks at me like I'm speaking a different language. One she doesn't understand.

"Matthew?" she says.

"Matthew Jordan," I say.

"Matthew Peter Jordan," Kai says.

She looks at us, and I can't tell if she's happy or sad or it's just that she has no idea what we're talking about. Then she turns around and shouts up the stairs, "Peter! Peter!"

We wait in silence, while an old man huffs and puffs down the stairs.

"What is it, Elizabeth?" he barks.

She points a shaking finger at us. "These boys ... they ..."

"What? Are they after my gnomes? Hands off, you louts."

"We're not louts," Kai says.

Mrs Jordan's mouth is wobbling. Her eyes are wet and her voice is wavery. "They ... they were asking about Matthew."

"Matthew?" Mr Jordan's hairy grey eyebrows shoot upwards. His mouth gapes. His eyes are wide open behind his thick specs.

"Matthew Peter Jordan," Kai says again, trying to be helpful.

"And what do you want with Matthew Peter Jordan?" the old man says.

"We were hoping you might be able to tell us something about him," I say. "About where he is now. About his life."

Two things happen when I say that. The old lady bursts into tears, pulls a tissue from her cuff and sobs into it. And the old man explodes with anger.

"Is this some kind of joke?" he roars. "Are you doing this on purpose? Because it's a pretty sick joke!"

"We didn't mean to upset you –" I say, shocked, but he's coming at me. He raises his hand and grabs my ear and sort of twists it, which is very, very painful.

"Ow!" I howl. "What?"

"Clear off!" he yells, in my other ear. "Go! And never come back."

"But we were just –"

"I don't want to hear it!" he bellows. "Look, it's one thing to nick my gnomes and litter the street. It's quite another to march up and ask my wife ... can't you see her heart is broken ... all these years and it still cuts like a knife ..."

"But we didn't ..." Kai never gets the words out.

Mr Jordan – who clearly needs anger management classes – grabs his ear too and marches the two of us to the front gate. "Get lost!" he shouts. "And never come back!"

12: THINK THROUGH YOUR LIES BEFOREHAND IF POSSIBLE

That was some encounter. We try to make sense of it on the way home. Was it a case of mistaken identity? Or did Mr and Mrs Jordan think we were trying to con them?

Or had my dad done something so awful that they'd totally disowned him?

Something to do with criminal gangs?

Something to do with protesting against animal testing, nuclear weapons and global warming?

Kai has some useless theories. Maybe my grandad is actually the boss of a massive company that pumped chemicals into the air and my dad protested against it for so long that it went bust?

"He was a bus driver," I say.

"Oh. OK." Even Kai's dad thinks buses are a good thing, especially the electric ones.

"Maybe he stole his dad's bus?"

"Shut up, Kai. It was more than that." I remember the old lady's face. Like we'd cursed her, spat in her face, peed on the gnomes. "Maybe he murdered someone," I say.

"Your dad, a murderer? That's mind-blowing – even for you."

"Maybe I should write to them ... Explain ..." I'm feeling bad about Mrs Jordan.

"Nah," Kai says. "We're playing the Barbarians again tomorrow. Let's see if Ball Dropper's dad turns up."

"Hagrid," I say.

"Butter Fingers."

End of conversation. Huh.

I get back home to find Mum and Jason in the kitchen. Waiting for me. Looking serious.

"River, have you been messing with Jason's files?" Mum starts.

I can't think what to say. This isn't like me.

"It wasn't me," I say. Lame.

"Then who was it?" Jason's voice is all calm and friendly, which is pretty freaky seeing as he thinks I've been snooping around his secrets. It's freaky and sinister.

I shrug. "Maybe a burglar?"

"A burglar?" Mum says. "But we've been here all day."

"I haven't," I say. I think about where I have been, and I feel sad and confused, all over again.

"Last night," Jason says. "When me and your mum went for a drink. Did you go through my stuff then?"

I get angry. "Look, I said it was a burglar, right? I was on the phone to Kai, and then I hear this noise. This *thud, thud, thud* noise. Someone coming up the stairs. And I assume it's you, OK? So I don't do anything. And then I hear someone on the landing. And there's this huge guy, really ugly, with a massive knife, OK? But he's got his back to me, and I just watch him go downstairs. *Thud, thud, thud.* And he lets himself out and I watch him run away. And I feel bad that I didn't stop him. But the knife was nasty."

"So," Jason says, still freakily calm. "He came into our house and looked in my files and then put everything back a bit mixed up but quite tidy? And he didn't bother to steal anything?"

"Look, I didn't ask him what he was doing, OK?" I say. "I didn't want him to carve me up. I don't expect you to care about that, but Mum might."

She raises an eyebrow. "And you never said anything about this last night or this morning?"

I think about telling her what I found out. How Jason is super rich. How he's got a file full of stuff about my dad.

I don't. I need to protect her.

"I didn't tell you because I thought you might be scared."

"Oh. Well. Thank you, River." She sighs. "I was on your side with that teacher, but this is ridiculous. I'm not standing for your lies any more."

I wish Jason would go away. This isn't a spectator sport. I don't need him to hear Mum getting angry at me.

"I used to think it was cute when you made up stories." Mum is almost ranting now. "I thought you had a good imagination. But now! You should know better, River. You're making a fool of yourself!"

"Look, Tanya –" Jason says.

Mum holds up a hand to stop him. "This is between me and River!" she shouts. "I have a right to a new life, River. I have a right to a new partner. You're nearly grown up. You're going to leave home one day. Can't you accept it? Jason's part of our family now!"

Jason tries again. "If I can just –"

I could have told him not to bother. When Mum explodes it's fireworks night.

"So, River," she yells, "you don't nose through Jason's stuff, you don't use his computer and you stop telling your stupid lies about everything! Got it?"

"All right!" I shout. "Leave me alone! I didn't want to worry you, that's all! Next time some guy with a knife breaks in, don't come crying to me!"

"Do you think we should call the police?" Jason says when at last I shut up.

Silence.

"There might be fingerprints," he adds.

"Whatever," I say.

"Jason ..." says Mum.

"It's OK," he says. "River, if you want to know about me or my work or if you want to use the computer, just check first, OK?"

"Call the police," I say. "Fingerprint away. I don't care."

13: THE TRUTH HURTS AS MUCH AS SOME LIES

Of course Jason insists on coming with me to football the next day. As he does every week. It's getting really annoying how Marcus lets him do the team talk and everyone laughs at his stupid jokes, soaks up his made-up facts and listens to his pathetic tactics.

I don't. I do everything the opposite of what Jason says. Which means that my team mates start swearing at me, and the Barbarians score two goals in the first ten minutes. And then Marcus subs me out.

"It wasn't my fault!" I rage, furious. "It was Jason's tactics!"

Marcus sighs. "I can't have my team wrecked because you're finding it difficult to accept your step-dad, River."

I go all cold inside. "What? Who said that?"

"It's obvious, River. He says go wide, you stay in the centre. He says send crosses over to Raffi, you keep the ball to yourself. I know it's not easy when your family changes, but he's a nice guy and he's making an effort. You're fifteen, not five. Grow up a bit, son. Now, shut up, watch and learn, and maybe I'll put you back on after half time."

I feel like Marcus has punched me in the gut. How dare he assume he knows about me and my family? He knows nothing. I walk as far away as I can from him and the other dads – Jason's running the line again – but not as far as the other team's supporters. Near enough to see them and near enough to hear them. Near enough to spot Hagrid's dad, and see his tattoo and listen to him chat to another Barbarian father.

"How's it going, Steve?" the other dad says. "Ollie like being in goal?"

So, his name is Steve. I think about going back to the old couple in Ilford.

Have you got another son called Steve? What's he like?

"Yeah, he does," my possible Uncle Steve says. "He's having a great time."

"He's certainly built for the job!" The other dad laughs, and after a pause Steve joins in.

"He's done OK so far," he says. "It's nice to be a winner."

I get the feeling that Hagrid the Hulk hasn't been a winner in many things.

"Too right," the other dad says. "This lot aren't causing much trouble, are they? Apparently they've got a new assistant manager who's shaken things up."

I look away. We've won every game since Jason got involved, but I'll never give him credit for that. In fact, if he hadn't interfered, we'd probably have an even better goal difference.

"I heard they won seven–nil last week," the bloke-who-might-be-my-uncle-Steve says.

"So," the other dad says, "how's life at the yard? Still making life safer for the rest of us?"

The yard? Is it some sort of scrap yard? But how would that make life safer for anyone?

"I'm mostly at a desk now," Steve says. "Boring stuff. Admin. Nothing interesting. Suits me just fine."

"River!" Marcus is calling me. I can see Raffi on the ground, holding his ankle, looking like he's about to be sick.

I jog back onto the pitch, trying to get my head back into the game. I don't even know what the score is.

But my brain is buzzing with new information.

Then it comes to me like a lightning strike.

The Yard is Scotland Yard.

Scotland Yard is the HQ of the Metropolitan Police. It's the home of London's police force.

My possible Uncle Steve could be a cop. A boring, desk-based cop, but still a cop.

So what does that make my dad?

14: SOMETIMES THINGS THAT SOUND LIKE LIES ARE TRUE

In the car on the way back, Jason drones on about the match. Who played well, who was poor, how did I think the Barbarians shaped up? It was a cup match and the score was 3–3, so we'll have to play them again. And again in the league too.

"Their goalie is good, isn't he?" Jason says. "He's got elastic arms. Couldn't believe it when he saved that shot of yours."

This is fake nice Jason, because my shot was rubbish and we both know it. Hagrid plucked it out of the air in his meaty paw no problem at all.

Ten awkward minutes later, and we're almost home when Jason's phone rings. He looks down to see who it is, says, "I need to take this," and switches on the hands-free.

"Sean! Hi!"

"Hey, Jason. Can you talk?"

Jason looks at me. "Yeah, yeah sure. Just driving River home from football."

"OK. Well. Those people I was telling you about? They're on for a meeting. Call me later and I'll give you the details."

"How about you message me?"

"Nah. Better in person. Why don't we have a pint later? Meet you at the Lion and Unicorn? Eight-ish?"

"Sure. See you then."

I sit there, thinking.

"What do you and Kai reckon to Sean?" Jason asks.

"He's one of my mum's oldest friends," I reply. "Unlike you."

"So, you think he's a good guy?"

"What do you care?" I remember the file on my dad. "Why are you snooping around, asking questions?"

"I thought you liked people asking questions."

"What makes you think that?" I say.

"Because you come up with great answers, River. Go on, tell me that Sean's really a brain surgeon, but he's not working right now because he's been accused of sleeping on the job."

"That's so crap," I mutter.

"You can do better, I'm sure."

"Are you saying I make things up?" As I say it, I realise how stupid I sound.

"I think that sometimes, when we're desperate for answers, we fill in the gaps for ourselves," Jason says. "I always used to. Like, when I missed people I would imagine what they were doing, what they were up to."

I'm saying nothing. No words, true or false, are coming out of my mouth.

"You know, you didn't have to go snooping in my office to find out about me," Jason says. "We could talk."

I want to get out of the car. But we're going quite fast.

"I didn't go snooping," I say. "It was a burglar."

"OK," says Jason. "But the police haven't caught him yet, so I'm putting extra bolts on the front and back doors." He turns to look at me. "You can help if you want."

"Nah, you're all right."

"Sure you trust me to do it?"

He has a point.

"I'll check your work afterwards," I say.

"OK," Jason says. "It's important we all feel safe at home."

I don't say anything in the hope he'll shut up. But no, nothing stops him.

"I think the burglar had a good look at my bank details," he says. "I'm a bit worried he might steal my identity. Take money out of my account."

"Are you calling him a thief?" I burst out.

"Well, he is just a random burglar."

"Well, actually, maybe he's not so random," I say. "Maybe he's investigating you. Maybe he's investigating why you say you're a journalist when you don't have a job. He's investigating where your money comes from. And why you're living in a crappy little house with me and my mum, when you own a flat in a dead posh area."

Jason whistles. "Do you think so? Well, maybe you're right. I am quite mysterious, after all. Secretive even."

I can't help but wonder where he's going with this. "What do you mean?" I ask.

"My work, it's not easy to explain," he says. "I'm a freelance investigative journalist for all sorts of newspapers and websites and magazines. Sometimes I don't use my own name."

"What? Why?"

"So I can find out the truth about people who have got something to hide, River."

"Is that why you've got so much money?" I ask him. "Enough to take five people to Costa Rica?"

"No," Jason says. "Have you ever thought about why I wanted to get married a long way from London?"

No. Of course I haven't.

"I have no family, River," he tells me. "My parents and my sister were killed in a car crash when I was twelve. My grandparents adopted me, but they're dead now. I was alone in the world, until I met your mum. And that's why I have money, that's why you and your mum mean so much to me, and that's why I've moved out of my flat and in with you two. If you see the burglar again, you can tell him that."

I'm shocked to find that I have a massive lump in my throat. If he's telling the truth, then I almost feel sorry for him. If he's lying – but who would tell lies like that?

And I remember him at the fake beach wedding. Making his stupid, boring speech. Talking about the people who couldn't be there. Saying, "Mum and Dad, Georgia, Gran and Grandpa. I miss you very much. I know you'd be so happy if you were here today."

At the time, I'd wondered why they hadn't flown out to Costa Rica as well.

Maybe Jason's not so fake after all?

Or has he made up this whole story to try and make me like him?

15: SOME TRUTHS ARE AS HARD TO SWALLOW AS LIES

Monday morning, I set off for school as usual. But I don't go to Kai's house. Instead I head for the tube station. It's like I'm in a trance. Before I know it I'm on the Central Line heading for Ilford.

Jason's story made me realise I haven't got any family either. Mum's only relatives are in New Zealand, and she doesn't keep in touch with them. And I don't know any of my dad's family. For obvious reasons.

Mr and Mrs Jordan could be my actual grandparents. I need to give them another chance.

So if I go by myself, and if I'm smart in school uniform, and if I'm very polite and the old lady is by herself, maybe she'll let me in. Maybe she'll talk to me.

I get all the way to the red front door and then my nerve fails me. So I sit down on the doorstep instead. She almost falls over me when she opens the door an hour later to let in the cat, a fat grey and black tabby who curls himself around my legs.

"He likes you," she says. "What are you doing, sitting on my step?"

I stand up.

"I came to say sorry for upsetting you the other day. And I wanted to explain, and show you something."

She looks me up and down. "Well," she says. "I suppose you could come in. Just for five minutes."

Their house isn't much bigger than ours, but it's so different. We have walls painted red, orange, pink and green. Big bold paintings that Mum did, wall hangings from India, painted bowls from Morocco. A squashy sofa, covered with throws. Bare wooden floorboards and a rag rug made from old jeans.

The Jordans' house has flowery wallpaper and a swirly carpet. The sofa and armchairs match and are a soft green. There's a fireplace and a shelf with some framed photos. Mr and

Mrs Jordan all dressed up at a party. Mr Jordan holding a small gold clock.

Mrs Jordan nods at that picture.

"My Peter," she says. "Thirty-five years' service on the buses. They gave him that clock on the mantelpiece."

"It's a very nice clock," I say, a bit helplessly.

"It is. It'd be a family heirloom if we had any family."

I spot my chance. "Mrs Jordan," I say. "I'm sorry I upset you the other day. Can I explain?"

"Go ahead," she says. "I'm listening."

"My name is River Jones. I've never met my dad. He left my mum before she knew she was pregnant."

"That's an unusual name," she says. "River."

I tell most people that I was named after the River Thames because my dad holds the world record for canoeing down it. But this time I tell the truth.

"My mum likes a song. It's called 'Cry Me a River'. I think she chose my name because she was kind of sad once my dad left."

"I know that song," says Mrs Jordan. "It's a favourite of mine too. Your poor mother, she must have had a hard time."

"No one knows why he left," I tell her. "They didn't row or anything, and she says he would have been happy about me if he'd known. But he didn't. He never came back. He even left his passport behind."

"That's strange," she says. "But what has this got to do with me?"

I take a breath. "His name was Matthew Peter Jordan," I tell her. "He was born on the 7th of March 1973. I sent away for a copy of his birth certificate. Look."

I pull my dad's birth certificate and passport out of my bag and hand them to her.

She looks at them in silence.

"So, you think this man is my son, Matthew, and that he's your dad. You think I'm your grandmother?"

I look at her, trying to see if she's like me at all. Her eyes are pale blue and her nose is long and thin. But there's something about the way she looks at me that's kind, and I like the way the cat rubs against her, confident that it's loved and welcome. It gives me hope.

"Yes," I say. "I'd like that."

She gets up. "Stay there," she says. "I've something to show you."

I sit and wait and look at the clock on the mantelpiece. It's a family heirloom. Will it be mine one day?

She comes back with a piece of paper in her hand. It looks like the birth certificate that I've just shown her.

"I'm very sorry, River. It's nice to meet you, and there's nothing I'd like better than to have a grandson. But it's just not possible."

She hands me the paper. It's not a birth certificate at all. It's the exact opposite.

It's a certificate of the death of Matthew Peter Jordan.

He died of pneumonia. In 1974. Here in this house.

He was only eleven months old.

16: SOME LIES ARE EVIL

I sit and look at the death certificate for what feels like an hour but is really only five minutes, according to the clock on the mantelpiece.

"I don't understand," I say. "How can they have the same name and the same birthday?"

"They can't," she says. She opens up my dad's passport at the photo page, and stabs a finger at his face. "I think he stole my baby's name," she says and I can hear anger in her voice. "I think he's gone around calling himself Matthew Peter Jordan, when he has no right to. I think that this person – your father – lied to your poor mother, and ran away before she could find out. Maybe he's still doing it now. Maybe he's still living our Matthew's life. Or maybe he's stolen some other dead baby's name."

The room has gone all blurry. Why would anyone do this? Why would my dad do this? That makes him worse than any ordinary liar. His lies weren't just stories. They were weapons.

And if he lied about his name and his birthday, then what do I know about him? Only that he had a snub nose and sandy hair. Only that he had a tattoo of a rose and a spider's web. Only that my mum thought he loved her.

A stupid tear splashes onto my hand. I look at Mrs Jordan and I see that she's crying too.

"It hurts, doesn't it?" she says. "It breaks your heart. My Matthew was a lovely baby. He had little dimples in his cheeks and he was very cheery, very happy. He never crawled, but he used to shuffle around on his bum. So comical he looked. So lovely."

She goes over to the fireplace and picks up a framed photo. A baby beams out at me. He has a curl in the middle of his head, and one tooth.

"Two weeks later he was dead," she says. "He didn't deserve to die, and he doesn't deserve this. He only had his name and our love. How can someone steal that away from him?"

I haven't got an answer. I'm thinking about Hagrid, the gigantic goalie. I'm thinking about his dad with his tattoo and his snub nose.

"I don't suppose you have a person called Steve in your family?" I ask. "A police officer? Works at Scotland Yard? Has a son called Ollie?"

She shakes her head, her eyes still full of tears. "No," she says. "Is he a friend of yours? Can he help us find out who did this?"

"No," I say.

I'm thinking hard. If my dad stole a dead baby's identity, then he did that for a reason. He didn't want anyone to know who he really was. Why would he do that? Is he a criminal?

Or a spy? Is that the sort of thing that a spy would do?

Could a police officer be like a spy?

I think again about Hagrid the Hulk. He must be about my age. An Under 16 team is meant to be for anyone born in the year from 1st September to 31st August, but in practice the best teams are full of the oldest boys in the year. My team is full of people with autumn birthdays. I bet the Barbarian team is too.

Maybe the Hulk's dad isn't actually his dad. Maybe he's a step-dad, like Jason wants to be to me.

But the Hulk and his dad both have the same sort of nose. And I have that nose too.

"Has this been a terrible shock?" Mrs Jordan says. Her voice jolts me out of a maze of questions. "Tell you what, I'll make a nice cup of tea and you can tell me a bit about yourself."

The tea is hot and sweet and sort of comforting. She gives me a big slice of ginger cake too. And when I tell her all about school and Mum and Jason and Kai, I stick to the truth.

It's all I've got left.

17: IF YOU'RE A KNOWN LIAR, NO ONE BELIEVES YOU WHEN YOU TELL THE TRUTH

"You know this airport in Kent?" says Kai.

It's Tuesday and it's break time and we're hanging around outside the staff room. Kai forgot to hand in his homework and I'm meant to be explaining why I was absent yesterday.

"Yeah," I say, but I'm not really listening. Who cares about airports when your dad is the sort of person who steals a dead baby's name and birthday and makes them his own?

Kai chunters on about bird life and noise and pollution and what Sean says about it all, and *blah blah blah*. I think about Hagrid the Hulk and his dad, and how and when I'm going to do anything about it. We play the Barbarians again on Sunday.

"So, I might miss the match," Kai says. "I need to think of a cover story for Bob."

"What?" I say. He clearly thinks he's explained something to me.

"A *cover story*. To explain why I'm not playing football."

"So, you're going to miss the match on Sunday?" I say. Bob the Builder always comes to support Kai.

"Duh, yeah." Kai pulls a face. "How can I be in two places at once? So what do I tell Bob and my mum?"

"Oh, I don't know. That you've sprained your ankle?"

Kai isn't impressed. "That's lame coming from you."

"Yeah, well, sorry, but I've got a lot on my mind," I say.

Of course I should tell Kai what happened, but somehow I can't. His real dad is a proper hero, saving the Arctic from evil oil companies. His step-dad is a builder and eats meat, but he's a nice guy and he likes Kai and he's straight down the line. My step-dad is probably a fake. My real dad is a liar *and* a fake. And he's possibly – but I can't even think about Hagrid's dad. *He* can't be my dad. He can't be.

Kai's teacher comes out and takes the Maths homework, and Kai asks if I want him to stay, but I say, "Nah, don't worry, it's OK."

"So, you want to do this protest with me?" he asks.

I have no idea what he's on about. "When is it again?" I ask him, to stall for time.

"Sunday! Look, don't tell anyone, will you? It's serious stuff. We could get arrested."

At last I'm listening. "Arrested? Whoa! What are you on about?"

Kai's got one of those faces that never really looks annoyed. He's always smiling. But right now he scrunches up his nose, and says, "Forget it." Then he marches off down the corridor.

Oh. I've said something wrong. I ought to go after him. But Mr Zakouri's just come out of the staff room.

"River," he says. "Come in." His office is small and airless and hot. He sits down and nods at a chair for me.

"So," he says. "Talk me through yesterday. Mown down by a runaway elephant? Kidnapped by a gang of bank robbers?"

I can't think of anything to say.

"Why don't you tell me the truth?" Mr Zakouri says.

Why not?

"I had to go and see someone," I start. "I thought she was my gran. But she wasn't. I think my dad might be a cross between a spy and a cop. I think he steals names from dead babies. I think he might have another son, the same age as me. And –"

Mr Zakouri holds his hand up to stop me.

"Enough!" he says and I see that he's glaring at me.

"But I –"

"You've done well in recent weeks, River," he says. "We all thought you'd stopped with the lies."

"Yes, but –"

"I thought we'd made some progress. Got through to you."

"Yes, but I –"

"Take a detention. You've let yourself down."

18: YOU CAN'T RUN AWAY FROM YOUR LIES

"So, how come Kai's not playing?" Jason asks me on the way to the match. "He knows how important this game is. We need to beat those Barbarians once and for all."

Six months ago, all I'd have been able to think about was the match ahead. Life was simpler then. Now, football is the last thing on my mind. I'm obsessing about him. Steve. Hagrid's dad. My dad.

He must be my dad.

The thought is almost unbearable. When I think about it my chest goes tight and I feel like I can't breathe. Blood booms in my ears. He can't be. He can't be.

We get to the pitch and Jason helps Marcus put the goals up and they talk tactics, and how they're going to cover for Kai's absence. He's improved a lot recently. He's a vital plank of our defence.

"How about you play in defence, River?" Jason asks. "I know you prefer midfield, but just this once?"

"OK," I say, as I lace my boots. "No problem." It's not as though I'm going to be on the pitch for long. I have a plan.

I play for fifteen minutes. That is, I loiter around in defence, watching the action, which is all taking place around Hagrid's goal. He saves one shot, another, and then Raffi takes a corner and Sonny boots it into the back of the net.

Hagrid didn't stand a chance. His cheeks go pink and his mouth turns down.

But then the whistle blows and the ball's coming my way. I put myself in front of their striker and go for the ball. It's not difficult to win it. It's also not difficult to fall over my own feet and lie there moaning on the ground like I've been fouled.

"River?" Jason's on the pitch with the first aid kit and my water bottle. "What happened?"

"Argh!" I cry. "I'm in agony! My ankle!"

I limp off, supported by Jason. Marcus gives me a look. "What happened there, River, fall over your own shadow?"

"I just twisted my ankle."

"Rest it. There's a bench over there if you want."

The bench is near the other side's supporters. If I limp over, I can put Part Two of my plan into action.

I sit on the bench and look for Steve. He's not chatting to anyone today. He's watching Hagrid, and checking his phone now and again.

Marcus and Jason are focused on the action. The other subs are way over the other side. No one will notice if I sidle over to the group of Barbarian dads.

"Anyone here got a grey BMW?" I ask them. "I saw a guy in the car park earlier, looked like he was scratching the bodywork."

Steve's head jerks up. "That could be my car. Where was it parked?"

"I'll show you," I say.

And just like that we're leaving the match, walking down the slope to the car park, side by side.

Me and him.

Me and Steve.

Me and the baby name thief?

Me and my dad?

My mouth's gone as dry as the desert where Jason claims he ran his marathon in the sand.

"That's my car – was it that one?"

I can't speak. I nod instead.

"It looks OK from here," he says, puzzled. "Can you show me where he was scratching it?"

Another nod.

"Cat got your tongue?" he asks.

"I ... I ... I've got something to ask you," I say.

"What's that?"

We've reached his car now and he's inspecting the bodywork. It's gleaming, spotless, perfect. Inside I can see an anorak, a boot bag, the Sunday papers. A headline. VIOLENCE FEARS AT AIRPORT MARCH.

"Can't see any damage," he says.

"You're a policeman, aren't you?" I manage to ask.

He raises an eyebrow. "I'm sorry, what?"

"You're a policeman. Have you always been a policeman?" My voice is shaking. "Can you tell me something?" I say. "Is it a crime to pretend to be someone else?"

"What is this?" Steve's frowning. His hands curl into fists.

"To steal a baby's identity?" I press on, reckless. "Is that a crime?"

"What the –?" He's staring at me. "You're not ... you look ..."

"River!" Jason's at my side. I'm not sure if I'm relieved or angry. "What's going on?"

"You tell me," Hagrid's dad says. "You tell me. Is this your kid? He told me he'd seen someone scratch my car. But it's fine and he's –"

"I'm not his kid," I say.

"Step-dad," says Jason.

"I never knew my dad," I say.

"Well, since my car's OK ..." Steve's backing away from us.

"I asked you a question," I say.

Jason looks at me. Then he looks at Steve. Really looks. Back and forth a few times – I can see him compare eyes, mouths, noses.

Then he says, "Does the name Matthew Jordan mean anything to you?"

Someone makes a weird, sighing sort of noise. I think it was me. Steve's mouth opens and closes. He looks at Jason. He looks at me, and blinks three times. One, two, three.

I think he's going to say something. But then he backs off, jumps into his shiny grey BMW and speeds out of the car park.

19: YOU NEED TO KNOW WHO YOU CAN TRUST

I don't know what to say. Jason doesn't either.

"Ankle feeling better then?" is the best he can do.

"Yes," I say. Then, "How did you know it was him? It was him, wasn't it?"

"Yeah," he says. "I'm pretty sure that was him. I'm sorry, River. What a total scumbag."

"What about Hagrid?" I say.

I imagine how Hagrid the Hulk will feel when he realises his dad has disappeared. That he's not watching him play football any more. My throat feels all shredded and bloody, like I've swallowed a bag of razor blades. And my eyes are sore and gritty. I rub them to try and make them feel better. It doesn't work.

"Hagrid?" Jason says.

"Their goalie. It's his … he's his … he was here because …"

"That's his son?" Jason shakes his head. "I didn't realise. I thought he'd tracked you down somehow."

"No. I tracked him down. Sort of."

"River," Jason says, "would it help to play the rest of the match? Or shall we go? If you limp like you mean it I could say I'm taking you to A&E."

I take a long, shuddering breath. "I want to play," I say. "I don't want to tell any more lies."

When we get back to the pitch it's the end of half time, and Marcus is looking pained – I guess he had to do the strategy talk. He swaps us around so I'm back in midfield. But I play like a three-legged donkey. I can't bear to look at Hagrid, his innocent eyes, his bulky torso, his chunky thighs.

'He's my brother,' I keep thinking, and then I want to vomit.

At last the ref blows the whistle. It's a draw, but at least we've survived the match. I know what's going to happen now. Because it's a cup match and because we've already played twice the ref says it's time for a penalty shoot-out.

We all gather round so Marcus can pick who will shoot first.

"Raffi," he says. "Max. Nathan. Sonny. And River."

"I can't," I say. "My ankle."

"You're all right," says Marcus. He's totally ruthless. He says his style as a manager is slightly to the right of Winston Churchill and Genghis Khan. "We need you," he tells me. "And we might have won by that point anyway."

I look at Jason and beg him with my eyes to stop this somehow. I can't stand in front of Hagrid and take a penalty kick against him. Against Ollie.

But Jason shakes his head and says, "If your ankle hurts, we'll understand if you miss. But you're a good footballer, River. You can do it."

I suppose his words are meant to boost my confidence, but they wash off me, meaning nothing. Out of the corner of my eye, I can see Ollie talking to his manager. He's looking around for his dad. He can't believe he's not there.

And suddenly I feel angry. Steaming, stabbing mad. My dad might not feel he owes me anything, and in fairness he never even knew about me. But he shouldn't abandon his real-life son Ollie half way through a cup match. When there could be a penalty shoot-out, which has to be every goalie's worst nightmare.

We go first. Raffi looks cool and relaxed, Ollie's sweating. Raffi saunters up, his foot almost strokes the ball, and bam! It's in the back of the net. Ollie gets up from the floor. He went totally the wrong way.

But now their forward is taking position, and his ball finds the spot too.

1–1.

Max takes the next one, and Hagrid – Ollie – gets a finger to it but he can't stop its path to the top left corner of the goal.

"Butter Fingers!" my team shouts. All except me. I don't know who I want to win any more. It's weird, but I don't want them laughing at Ollie.

2–2.

And then Nathan scores and their player misses.

Sonny sends his shot straight over Ollie's head. Ollie's cheeks are bright pink and sweat is trickling down his nose. If they miss this time, we've won. But they don't. The shot deflects off the goal post and tricks our goalie into diving the wrong way.

4–3.

The game is mine to win. If I blow it, then we might still win – but if I score the game is definitely ours. They're crushed, they're beat, the mighty Barbarians humbled. I try and look confident as I walk towards the spot.

And then I think how horrible it'll be for Ollie if we win. Will they all give him a hard time? Will he take the blame?

The ball's in place. I take a short run, my foot goes back and WHAM! The ball flies through the air and smashes into the back of the net. He didn't even get near.

My team whoops, runs up to me, hugs me and shrieks and cheers. I'm in the middle of the crowd. My back starts to ache from the slaps of congratulations.

And Ollie takes off his gloves, scoops up the ball, holds it to his chest and trudges off the field.

I watch to see if the Barbarians tell him it's not his fault, put their arms around him, slap him on the back.

They don't. They really are Barbarians.

I take off, running towards him. I hold out my hand. "Bad luck," I say. "You had the sun in your eyes. That always makes it difficult."

He shakes my hand. His feels plump and clammy.

"Ollie," one of the dads says. "I'm giving you a lift. Your dad texted me – he had to go."

"Where do you live?" I ask, straight up.

Ollie gives me a startled look. "Finchley," he says. "Right by North Finchley station."

"Ah," I say. "Good to know."

20: LIES CAN TRAP YOU. LIES CAN MAKE YOU DO STUPID STUFF

We get in the car and Jason says, "Well done," and then he asks if Ollie seemed OK.

"Yes," I say and then, "No. I don't know. His team weren't being very supportive."

"It's hell being a goalie," Jason says. "I did it for a year. Escaped to defence in the end. Are you OK?"

I open my mouth and then close it again. I'm not OK and I have a heap of questions for him. How did he know who my dad was? What's the file on his computer all about?

"Yes," I say, and then, "No. I mean yes. I mean no."

"OK," he says. "Let's not talk now. Later. I've got a lot to tell you, but only if you're in the right frame of mind. When you're ready."

He switches on the radio. We listen to classical music for a while – it's oddly calming – and then the news comes on. There's been a protest at the Department of Transport. People throwing smoke bombs and getting arrested and being kettled, whatever that is.

And I remember Kai asking me to come with him to something that was much more important than football, but he couldn't tell me what it was.

"Jason?" I say.

He turns the radio down.

"Did they say there was fighting? Trouble? At that protest?"

"They did."

"It's just ... Kai might be there."

"Kai?"

"He was listening to Sean at the barbeque, and talking like he wanted to do something. Direct action, he said."

"And you think he might have been caught up in this protest?"

"I don't know," I tell him. "His mum's away and he told Bob he was staying with me. But he's not."

"We should go down there," Jason says. "Find him."

"Please," I say.

Jason looks at me. "Are you OK? Have you got any clothes to change into?"

"No," I say. "I mean yes. I've only got my kit, but I'm OK. What does kettled mean?"

"They surround the protesters. Pen them in to keep them in one place. They don't let them out."

"What if the protesters need the loo?"

He shakes his head. "Tough luck."

"What if they're hungry?" I ask, but I know the answer.

"Kai strikes me as a sensible lad," says Jason.

"Yeah, but he's been getting more and more angry about stuff," I tell Jason. "About how no one listens. Politicians and big business and everyone. And he's cross with his mum for not being active any more, not being a protester. He really likes stories of the old days when they were all getting arrested and camping out in trees and everything. Kai –" I swallow – "he likes life to be dramatic. He likes action. He wants to be a big hero – like his dad."

"But would he do anything properly stupid?" Jason asks. Then he thumps the steering wheel. "Sean's an idiot. I should've talked to Kai about him."

"Why didn't you?"

"I was trying to find out what he was up to," Jason says. "I didn't think you'd appreciate it if I interfered in your friendships."

"Oh. No. True."

"Are you worried he'd do anything really dangerous, River?" Jason asks.

I remember Kai's face when Sean was talking. About hitting people where it hurt. About making them listen. About fighting to the bitter end.

"You were talking to Sean," I say. You had a drink with him."

"I know, but he was wary of me –"

"What do you mean?"

"OK, River." Jason sighs. "Here's the truth. As you know, I'm a journalist. I've been investigating people like Sean, people who wind other people up, get other people into trouble."

"You what?"

"People like Sean encourage direct protest, but they don't take part. They know all about a plan, but they never get into trouble. Some of them are just like that. But others, they're *agents provocateurs*."

"I don't do French," I say. "What does that mean?"

"It means someone who encourages other people to commit a crime, so that they get arrested and punished," Jason says. "A lot of the time, they're government agents. Governments in Russia, America, Britain, France, Canada have all used them against union members, protestors, anyone who poses a threat to the state."

"Does the government use them in Britain?" I ask. I'm finding it hard to make sense of what Jason's telling me. It sounds like a mad conspiracy theory.

"They have done at different times in history," Jason says. "But I think the police use them too. That's what I've been investigating."

I open my mouth to ask more. But then my phone beeps and I see that Kai's snapchatted me. A photo of Big Ben, the Houses of Parliament. And a frantic message.

RIVER HELP ME NOW. I DON'T WANT TO DO THIS.

21: SOMETIMES THE TRUTH FEELS LIKE A FILM. LIKE A STORY

"Where are you? What's up?"

Kai's on the phone and he's kind of not talking, kind of crying, kind of hysterical.

"I've got, I've got, I've got," he sobs into the phone and then Jason takes it from me.

"Kai, calm down," he says. "It's OK. We're going to sort this out."

"I've got a gun," Kai says and something in me freezes so cold, so tight that I don't think I'll ever be able to speak again. "They want me to ... They said ... They, they ..."

"Where are you?" Jason asks.

"They want me to shoot," Kai sobs. "At a tourist bus. On a tourist bus. They want me to."

He's not making sense.

"Who?" I scream. "Who wants you to?"

"We're coming," Jason says. "Don't get on any buses. Find a police officer. Tell them an extremist group is controlling you."

"I can't," Kai says. "They're watching. They'll shoot me."

"Kai, they won't. They can't."

"This guy. He was a sniper. In the army. He'll shoot me. He will."

"Kai, he's lying!" I shout, but Jason mouths "No!" at me.

"Where are you, Kai?" he says again. "We're coming. We're nearly there."

I look out the window and see that we're driving towards the Houses of Parliament. We're on the road by the Thames. And then I see him. All wrapped up in his hoodie. He's fidgeting and shaking and looking a lot like a little kid who wants to go to the loo and can't quite hold it in. He's looking around, twisting his head to see behind him, waiting and shaking and –

"Go!" Jason yells. He drives past a No Entry sign, makes a sharp turn and stops right by Kai.

Kai takes one startled look at my face and dives into the back.

Jason backs out. I'm aware of people screaming and yelling, of Kai's jagged breath, the noise of him throwing up all over the back seat, the stink of vomit, and then Jason slows down, stops, looks up at a police officer standing by the car.

"You went through a No Entry sign," she says.

"My boy was taken ill," says Jason.

The police officer looks at the pool of vomit in the back of the car. She wrinkles her nose.

Kai barfs again. Carrots and peas in a toxic orange colour.

"On your way," the police officer says.

We drive and drive, and at last I realise we're not heading for home. This isn't east London. This is somewhere greener and prettier, somewhere with big cars and driveways and front doors painted murky greens and blues.

Jason pulls over to the kerb and gets out a key. "Come on," he says to Kai. "Let's get you cleaned up."

22: SOMETIMES YOU HAVE TO LIE.
TO PROTECT THE INNOCENT

The flat Jason leads us into is all white walls and grey furniture, polished wood floors and a shiny bathroom. I recognise it from the estate agent's details I saw in Jason's office.

He gives Kai a towel and says, "You'll feel better after a shower. I'll hunt out some clothes."

"What about the gun?" I say.

Kai unzips his hoodie.

Jason holds out his hand. "Give it here."

Kai hesitates.

"It's OK," Jason tells him. "I know about guns. And no one was following us. I looped us all over the place."

"Where even is this?" I ask.

"It's my flat. Well, not for long. It's all ready to sell."

I look around. Two million quid! "Why would you leave here to live with us?" I ask.

Jason shrugs. "No idea. Why would I? I must be an idiot. Go and clean yourself up, Kai. You can put that robe on when you're done."

I sit on the sofa and drink lemonade and think about how Jason must love Mum a lot to leave this place and come and live in a maisonette in the grottier end of Finsbury Park.

All this time Jason's sitting at the shiny kitchen counter, looking at the gun. "It's a replica," he says after a bit. "A fake. Although poor Kai didn't know that."

"So why would they give Kai a fake gun?"

"So he could cause a diversion. So they could do something else ... All the action was at the Department of Transport, but they sent Kai down to the Houses of Parliament, to get the police running over there. Hmmm."

"What are you thinking?" I ask.

"I'm thinking maybe Sean isn't an *agent provocateur* at all. Maybe he's for real."

Then Jason gets out his phone and has a long, involved conversation with the police. By the time Kai's out of the shower and we're all eating pizza in front of the TV, there's a news report about a security alert at the Houses of Parliament. Three people have been arrested on terrorism charges.

"They'll be here soon," Jason says. "The police. It's OK, Kai. Just tell them you were there for the protest and they forced you to take the gun. That's true, isn't it?"

Kai looks at him and, after a long moment, he shakes his head.

"I wanted to be a hero," he says, and he can't meet our eyes. "I wanted to have an exciting life, things to tell people. Like Dad. Like Sean. Like River."

"My stories are all bollocks," I tell Kai and I think he's going to burst into tears or vomit again.

"I wanted to impress my dad," Kai says. "So he wouldn't be angry with me for flying to Costa Rica. You're lucky, River. You don't even know your dad ..."

"Sometimes you have to leave bits out of your story," Jason interrupts. "Think how your mum would feel if you were in big trouble. Be a hero for her. You need to say they forced you to take the gun."

Kai nods. "OK, Jason," he says in small voice. "They said they'd shoot me if I didn't do what they said. But I wanted to … I wanted to do something big. Something that would change things –"

"I knew Sean was up to something," Jason says, "but I didn't think he'd sink so low as to recruit a kid."

"It wasn't Sean," Kai says. "It was people on the internet. I never even met them before."

"But why, Kai?" Jason asks. "Why do something so extreme?"

Kai runs his fingers through his hair, and I answer for him.

"He wanted to be a real eco-warrior."

Jason's about to say something when the entry phone buzzes. It's the police – a man and a woman – and they talk to us and they talk to Jason and they talk to Kai. They're in normal, ordinary clothes. They look us in the eye and they thank us for our help. They say they'll want to talk to Kai again, with his mum present, but that he's not to worry. It's unlikely that he'll face any charges. After all, he hasn't actually done anything. Not quite.

"Three armed extremists, arrested thanks to you," the woman says.

"That makes you a hero if you ask me," says the man.

I really want to ask them a whole heap of questions.

Question 1. "Do you know a man called Steve at Scotland Yard?"

Question 2. "Do you know why he pretended to be called Matthew Jordan?"

Question 3. "Was he working for the police when he did that?"

Question 4. "What was Steve / Matthew trying to do?"

But, most of all –

Question 5. "Was he for real? Or was he an *agent provocateur*?"

23: YOU KNOW IT'S TRUE WHEN IT MAKES SENSE

It's been dark for hours by the time we get home, and the police are at Kai's house talking to his mum about Sean, about the internet, about everything, so he gets to stay over at ours. I'm pleased to have him here, and I'm pleased I don't have to stay up late thinking about that moment when Steve drove away from me in his flash car. My dad – my real dad.

I don't want to think about that moment when I smashed the ball past Ollie either. My half-brother – my brother.

Kai's gone when I wake up in the morning. I go downstairs and find Mum and Jason drinking coffee in the kitchen. I look around our cramped kitchen, the cupboard doors Mum painted turquoise and pink, the cork tiles peeling off the floor and think about Jason's sleek, modern, shiny kitchen.

He's chosen here. He's chosen us. And I've been really horrible to him.

"Kai's gone," Mum says. "Lorna's taken him home. She's in bits about what's happened. What was Kai thinking?"

"He thought he was acting for a good cause," Jason says.

"So did I, once upon a time," Mum says. "And the cause *is* good. But it's no excuse for violence. Those people that Kai met up with, they had explosives! Promise me never ever to do anything so stupid, River."

I promised her this about fifty times last night, so I ignore her.

"River, we owe you an explanation," Jason says. He knows better than to fight Sean's corner with Mum fierce like that. "And an apology. We know – I know – a lot more about your dad than we've told you. I just hadn't found him. But you did, and now I've put the final pieces together."

So Jason tells me. How he'd been investigating a story about undercover police agents who wormed their way into environmental groups. How they adopted the identities of dead children and talked people into taking direct action. So the protesters were arrested, put away where they couldn't cause any more trouble, and the police just drifted back to their real lives.

"You could have told me," I say. "After all, he is my dad."

Mum comes and sits next to me and takes my hand.

"Jason, do you mind if I talk to River by myself?" she says. "There are things I need to say."

"Sure," Jason says. "I've got work to do. The *Guardian*'s going to run with the story."

Mum waits until he's upstairs. Then she says, "You need to understand how I felt when Jason told me the truth. Imagine, River. The man I loved, the father of my child, never really existed. He lied to me, tricked me. He told me he loved me, he slept with me, and all the time he was telling me lie after lie after lie."

I swallow, hard. She must hate him so much now. What if she hates me too?

"I felt like I'd been –" She hesitates. "– Assaulted. It was a lot to make sense of, to process. I was upset, angry, confused. And Jason helped me sort it all out in my head. He listened. He put me in touch with other women in a similar position."

"Other women?" I can't believe it. "He did this to *other* women?"

Mum shakes her head. I watch her earrings bob up and down against her curls, like little silver boats on a black sea.

"Not him," she says. "But he wasn't the only police officer working undercover. There were a few of them."

"Do you hate him?" My voice isn't much more than a whisper.

She tries to smile at me, but neither of us can quite meet the other's eye.

"It's so hard, River," she says, and she twists the bangles on her wrist. "I can't hate Matthew Jordan. But I do hate Steve Greig."

That's his name. Steve Greig. His real name.

"Do you wish you'd never met him?"

"I could never wish that," she says. "Because that would mean I'd never have had you. And you're the best thing that ever happened to me."

"I am? Not Jason?"

"You are." Mum takes my hand in hers. "Jason is wonderful, and I know I can trust him. And there's nothing he wants more than to be a part of our family. Will you let him, River?"

I nod. "He's not so bad," I say and I squeeze Mum's hand.

24: I'M TELLING THE TRUTH, BUT I'M ALSO TELLING STORIES

My dad's real name is Steven Michael Greig. He was director of digital strategy for the Metropolitan Police. He lived in Chelmsford, just outside London, with his second wife and their twin daughters.

That was until Jason's story appeared in the *Guardian*, and then everywhere else. Then Steve Greig was suspended from his job, and my mum and two other women announced that they were suing the police for damages.

Mum's been in all the papers. She's been on television. She's fierce and proud, angry and strong, telling the story of how she was treated, making the point again and again that the state – represented by Steve Greig – lied and lied to her, invaded her home, her life and her body, and fathered her child. The Jordans have been interviewed too. Everyone knows the truth. Everyone knows what he did.

It's been exhausting. I know everyone's talking about me. But this time I'm not telling any stories about anything to anyone.

Mr Zakouri apologised for not believing me, which was nice of him, and said I could talk to the school counsellor if I want to. I don't.

There's only one person I want to talk to about what's happened.

The Barbarians train up in Finchley, at a swanky club with its own bar and changing rooms. The U16s have Wednesday nights, from seven till eight. I hang around outside the club, hood up, head down. I'm waiting for Ollie.

He's one of the last ones out. It looks like he's walking home on his own. I walk behind him for a while, till it's just the two of us, under the orange light of the lamp-posts.

He turns around. "Are you following me?"

He shouldn't be scared – he's way bigger than me – but I can see how his eyes are wide and his breathing is shallow.

I stick out my hand. "I'm River," I say.

"Oh. It's you."

"I'm sorry," I say. "I'm sorry about your dad."

"Apparently he's your dad too," Ollie says.

"Yeah." I pause. "Which makes us brothers."

"Half-brothers."

"Yeah. Half-brothers."

"I've got two half-sisters already," Ollie says. "They don't look like me. They're all blonde and pretty and cute."

"No one's ever called me cute," I say. "Or pretty. Or blonde, come to that."

All of a sudden, he grins. It makes me realise how serious his face is normally.

"I can't believe my dad did that," Ollie says. "It's just bizarre. He's so straight. So boring, even. I can't believe he was a hippy and had dreads and all that stuff."

"I can't believe it either," I say, "and I don't even know him."

"Do you want to know him?"

I shrug. "Not really. I'll never forgive him for what he did to my mum. And to the people whose baby's name he stole."

"It was beyond wrong," Ollie says. "Dad told me his bosses arranged it all. And he got sucked into being this new person, this different person, and it was confusing and difficult to live as a liar. But I can't really forgive him. And my mum, well, she gave up on him years ago. Now she doesn't even want me to see him.

"I can't forgive him," I say. "I never want to see him again."

We look at each other and then it's like we both decide to change the subject at the same time, because Ollie says, "That was a good penalty you took," and I say, "I'm sorry about that goal," and then we start comparing the Barbarians and my team, and then we find that we've walked together to his house.

"Come and meet my mum," he says.

But I'm worried about what she'll think and what I'll say to her. "Another time, mate," I say. "I'd better get the bus."

We swap phone numbers. We agree we'll go to Nando's together sometime soon.

And I go home. And Mum is there, and Jason – who isn't a fake and who isn't an enemy and who actually knows a lot of cool stuff. He's been telling me all about the marathon he ran in the Sahara. It's called the Marathon de Sables, and it's six times as long as other marathons, and you sleep in tents made out of goats' hair and you have to carry everything you need on your back. It's called the Toughest Foot Race on Earth, and Jason says we can train together and do it when I'm 18.

And he's also told me a lot about the history of undercover *agents provocateurs*. All I can say is that a lot of people have behaved really badly all over the world for a long, long time.

I go up to my room and I get out the book that Mr Zakouri gave me. *The Liar's Handbook*, I called it. I look at some of the stuff I've written. My so-called rules of lying.

And then I draw a line under it all and start to write.

ABOUT THE LIAR'S HANDBOOK

River and Tanya's story is a work of fiction. But I was inspired to write it by a real-life fight for truth and compensation. A group of women, who were members of political and environmental activist groups, discovered that men they'd had relationships with were in fact undercover police officers.

The Metropolitan Police has never admitted a deliberate policy of encouraging these relationships. But they have paid compensation to several women out of court, and have lost a claim for damages in the High Court made by another woman.

In November 2015, Assistant Commissioner Martin Hewitt of the Metropolitan Police said the relationships had been "wrong" and were a "gross violation of personal dignity and integrity". The women said the apology would "never make up for what we have endured", and they pointed out that no apology was made to those children fathered by the undercover police officers.

An official Inquiry into undercover policing was announced in 2015. Its chairman, Sir Christopher Pitchford, said, "The Inquiry's priority is to discover the truth."

Keren David

ABOUT KEREN DAVID

Keren David is an "author of empathy and truthfulness" whose prize-winning novels explore identity, love and family dynamics. Keren started her working life as a messenger girl making coffee and running errands at a newspaper before going on to be a reporter, political correspondent and editor-in-chief.

'Life-affirming, witty and uplifting ... David gets better with every book' – Daily Mail on Salvage

Our books are tested
for children and young people by
children and young people.

Thanks to everyone who consulted on
a manuscript for their time and effort in
helping us to make our books better
for our readers.